# ERIC CARLE

# The Foolish Tortoise

## Written by Richard Buckley

**LITTLE SIMON**

New York  London  Toronto  Sydney  New Delhi

A tortoise, tired of being slow,
Impatient to get up and go,

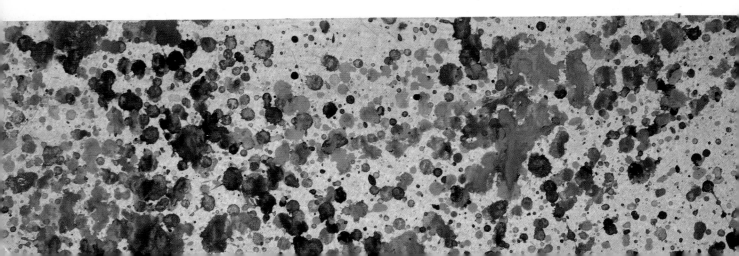

Took off his large and heavy shell
And left it lying where it fell.

"Hooray!" he cried. "Now I've been freed—
I'll see the world at double speed!"

Though faster, he was not express
And his protection was far less,
So when he heard a hornet's drone
The tortoise crept beneath a stone.

A hungry bird came swooping past,
He looked so fierce and flew so fast,
The tortoise hid behind some trees
And felt quite weak behind the knees.

"I don't feel safe, there's too much risk.
 If only I could be more brisk!"
 He headed for the riverbed:
 A fish swam up, the tortoise fled.

Along his way our hero went
And almost had an accident.
A snake with open jaws slid near.
The tortoise backed away in fear.

A hare, a hound, a horse raced by—
So rapidly, they seemed to fly.
The tortoise gasped, sat goggle-eyed—
"I'll never be that quick," he sighed.

He wandered on, the sun rose high.
"I wish I had more shade!" he cried.
A sudden thunderstorm swept in,
And soaked the tortoise to the skin.

The wind rose up, and soon the breeze
Was bending branches in the trees.

The tortoise shivered. "Now I'm cold.
I wish I hadn't been so bold."

"I think I've lost the urge to roam,
I think it's time that I went home.
Without my shell I don't feel right."
So when his shell came into sight,

He climbed back in and said,
"Good night!"

LITTLE SIMON

An imprint of Simon & Schuster Children's Publishing Division
1230 Avenue of the Americas, New York, New York 10020
Text copyright © 1985 by Richard Buckley
Illustrations copyright © 1985 by Eric Carle
Originally published in 1985 by Picture Book Studio
First Little Simon book and CD edition 2013. Also available in a Simon & Schuster Books for Young Readers
hardcover edition and a Little Simon board book edition.
All rights reserved, including the right of reproduction in whole or in part in any form.
LITTLE SIMON is a registered trademark of Simon & Schuster, Inc., and associated colophon is a trademark
of Simon & Schuster, Inc.
For information about special discounts for bulk purchases, please contact Simon & Schuster Special Sales
at 1-866-506-1949 or business@simonandschuster.com.
The Simon & Schuster Speakers Bureau can bring authors to your live event. For more information or to
book an event contact the Simon & Schuster Speakers Bureau at 1-866-248-3049 or visit our website at
www.simonspeakers.com.
Eric Carle's name and logo are registered trademarks of Eric Carle.
For more information about Eric Carle and his books and products, please visit: eric-carle.com.
For information about The Eric Carle Museum of Picture Book Art, please visit: carlemuseum.org.
Designed by Laura L. DiSiena
Manufactured in China 1212 SCP
First Edition
10 9 8 7 6 5 4 3 2 1
ISBN 978-1-4424-6638-8